Little Explorer, Big World

A BILINGUAL BOOK 双语故事书
English • Chinese Pinyin 英语 • 中文 拼音版

的纽约历险记

By 作者 **KIKE CALVO**

Illustrated by 插画 **WALTER CARZON**

Foreword by 序言 **Carl Safina**

"A mi pequeña exploradora, Pilarcita, que desde que nació, me ayudó a ver la vida, el mundo y la fotografía con nuevos ojos. ¡Nunca dejes de soñar!" — Kike Calvo.

"A Lucía, mi hija y dibujante preferida, que siempre me inspira con su imaginación." — Walter Carzon.

Scan & Listen
Dual language book: Scan or visit
www.littleexplorerbigworld.com
to download your FREE audio book.
Use code: **PILI**

扫描 & 听故事
双语故事书: 扫描或访问
www.littleexplorerbigworld.com
下载你的免费有声书
使用密码: **PILI**

The Adventures of

Pili

in New York

的纽约历险记

Author 作者: **Kike Calvo**

Illustrations 插画: **Walter Carzon**

Color Art 色彩艺术: **Silvana Brys**

Design 设计: **Sergio Sandoval**

English Translation 英语翻译: **Clara Rowe**.

Mandarin Translation 中文翻译: **Zeting Chen** 陈泽婷

Project Manager and Development 产品经理与开发: **Kike Calvo**

Content Editor 内容编辑: **John Matthew Fox**

Editor 编辑: **Vivienne Caballero**

Thank you to Shiyu Shen, Shuying Chen, Yuer Cui, and Hui Ye for their help reviewing the Mandarin translation.

非常感谢申诗雨、陈淑颖、崔月儿以及叶卉对我们的中文译文提供的帮助！

Learn more:

www.littleexplorerbigworld.com

www.waltercarzon.com

www.kikecalvo.com

FOREWORD

A little girl travels the world. Her Dad is a photographer. So though she is small—her life is big, encompassing everything from New York City to Colombia's wild rainforest.

By observing and listening, by thinking and by feeling—and probably because she has inherited a bit of her father's special ability to really see things—little Pili comes to care about nature, about people who speak other languages, and about peace.

Pili imagines a peaceful place in the world for children. Her plan: it will be a forest reserve, and it will be in Colombia. This is not an easy goal for a little girl to accomplish. But Pili is determined; somehow, she *will* get this done!

Now, the thing is, this book isn't too far from the real truth. Pili is a real girl, and her Dad is the author of this book. And the forest—they're making progress.

The children of the world—and little girls in particular—can use a few positive messages that will inspire them to aspire. This book has many such messages, tucked into a sweet, beautifully illustrated near-to-life narrative like little folded love-notes.

~ Carl Safina

Endowed Professor for Nature and Humanity, Stony Brook University
Founder, The Safina Center
Author, *Beyond Words; What Animals Think and Feel*

$\mathcal{P}$ili lived in New York, but often traveled the world with her father Kikeo, photographing wild animals, forests, and people from different cultures.

"Your house looks like a museum," her friends would say. "When can we explore it?"

Pili loved the people and places she visited with her father, like Cuba and China. But her favorite place was Colombia. She began to dream that someday one of her ideas could make the world a better place.

$\mathcal{P}$ili 住在纽约，但她经常和她的爸爸 Kikeo一起环游世界，拍摄着野生动物、森林和来自不同文化的人们。

"你们家看起来就像是一个博物馆，"她的朋友告诉她。"我们什么时候可以去探索一下呢？"

Pili 很喜欢那些和爸爸一起旅行过的地方和途中遇到的人们，比如古巴和中国。但她最喜欢的地方还是哥伦比亚。她梦想着有一天她能让世界变得更美好。

"Why are you always drawing in your notebook?" some children at school would say. "We do not understand why you sing in other languages or why you are always eating vegetables you grow in your garden."

One day, Pili saw an announcement for a contest for children: "Can you change the world?"

wèi shén me nǐ zǒng shì zài nǐ de bǐ jì běn shàng huà huà zài xué xiào de yì xiē xiǎo
"为什么你总是在你的笔记本上画画？"在学校的一些小
péng yǒu cháng cháng wèn tā
朋友常常问她。

wǒ men bù míng bai wèi shén me nǐ yào yòng qí tā yǔ yán chàng gē wèi shén me nǐ zǒng shì
"我们不明白为什么你要用其他语言唱歌，为什么你总是
chī zì jǐ jiā yuàn zi lǐ zhòng de shū cài
吃自己家院子里种的蔬菜。"

yǒu yì tiān kàn dào le yí gè miàn xiàng xiǎo péng yǒu de bǐ sài tōng gào nǐ kě
有一天，Pili 看到了一个面向小朋友的比赛通告："你可
yǐ gǎi biàn zhè ge shì jiè ma
以改变这个世界吗？"

"What can I do to make the world a better place?" she asked herself over and over.

"I know! I want to create a forest in Colombia for the children of the world. It will be a peaceful place where children can learn to love and protect nature," Pili said. "Now, I just need to think of creative ways to collect the money I'll need for the forest."

"If I win this contest, kids at school won't laugh at my ideas anymore," thought Pili. "Everyone will want to come and visit!"

"我能做些什么让世界变得更美好呢？"她一遍又一遍地问自己。

"我知道了！我想为全世界的小朋友们在哥伦比亚创造一片森林。那将会是一个充满和平的，让小朋友们学着去热爱和保护大自然的地方，" Pili 说，"现在我只需要开动脑筋，想办法筹集创造森林需要的资金就好啦！"

"如果我赢了这场比赛，学校里的小朋友们就再也不会嘲笑我的想法了，" Pili 想着，"大家都会想来瞧一瞧！"

Pili visited the New York Ballet, where she set up a lemonade stand.

She went to the Brooklyn Bridge, where she sold pictures she had drawn of her dream forest.

And on Coney Island, she cleaned up the beach, with the help of her drone, collecting cans and bottles she could recycle.

在纽约芭蕾舞团旁，Pili 摆了一个柠檬水小摊。

在布鲁林克大桥上，她卖了自己画的画，画中是她梦想的森林。

在康尼岛，她在无人机的帮助下清理了海滩，收集了一些能循环利用的瓶瓶罐罐。

Pili was walking home with her piggy bank when it started raining very hard. She liked to dance and jump in the rain with her rubber boots, even though she was always scolded when she did.

"When I am happy, I have to sing and dance!" Pili would say.

dāng   bào zhe tā de cún qián guàn wǎng jiā lǐ zǒu de shí hòu   yǔ tū rán xià dà le
当 Pili 抱着她的存钱罐往家里走的时候，雨突然下大了，
tā xǐ huan chuān zhe tā de xiǎo yǔ xuē zài yǔ zhōng bèng bèng tiào tiào   jí shǐ tā jīng cháng yīn wèi
她喜欢穿着她的小雨靴在雨中蹦蹦跳跳，即使她经常因为
zhè yàng zuò bèi zé mà
这样做被责骂。

wǒ kāi xīn de shí hòu   yí dìng yào chàng gē tiào wǔ   shuō guò
"我开心的时候，一定要唱歌跳舞！" Pili 说过。

But today was different. Just as she was about to jump over one of the puddles, Pili saw a scared little puppy that was in trouble. She knew she had to help.

As she raced toward the puppy, her piggy bank slipped out from under her arm. It rolled down the street and was swept into the river.

但今天有点不一样。正当她准备跳过一个水坑时，Pili
看到了一只遇到麻烦而瑟瑟发抖的小狗。她知道她必须要
帮助它。

当她跑向小狗时，她的存钱罐从怀里滑了下来，沿着街
道滚进了小河。

Back at home, Pili was happy because she had helped an animal in danger. But she was also sad since she had lost the piggy bank that held her savings for the forest.

huí dào jiā hòu　　　　gǎn dào hěn kāi xīn　　yīn wèi tā bāng zhù le yì zhǐ yù
回到家后，Pili 感到很开心，因为她帮助了一只遇
dào wēi xiǎn de xiǎo dòng wù　　dàn tóng shí tā yě hěn nán guò　　yīn wèi diū le zhuāng
到危险的小动物；但同时她也很难过，因为丢了装
zhe sēn lín zī jīn de cún qián guàn
着森林资金的存钱罐。

"I will name you Chimichurri," Pili said to her new friend.

Pili decided she would not give up. She told the kids at school about her project and invited them to join in. But they said her forest was a silly idea.

wǒ jiù jiào nǐ　　　　　　ba　　　　　　　duì tā de xīn péng yǒu shuō
"我就叫你 Chimichurri 吧！" Pili 对她的新朋友说。

tóng shí　　　　jué dìng bú fàng qì tā de sēn lín mèng xiǎng　　tā bǎ jì huà gào sù le xué xiào lǐ de
同时，Pili 决定不放弃她的森林梦想。她把计划告诉了学校里的

xiǎo péng yǒu men　　bìng qiě yào qǐng tā men jiā rù　　dàn tā men rèn wéi zhè ge sēn lín jì huà shǎ shǎ de
小朋友们，并且邀请他们加入。但他们认为这个森林计划傻傻的。

Pili wanted to win the contest more than anything in the world. So she went back to her desk and sketched out a new plan.

But it was too late. The day after she lost her piggy bank was the last day of the contest.

Pili 非常想赢得这次比赛。所以她回到书桌前，又花了好几个小时重新制定了一个计划。

但已经太晚了，因为这天就是能参赛的最后一天了。

One day, without any explanation, hundreds and hundreds of letters began to arrive at her house. Each envelope said: "To Pili, the little explorer."

yǒu yì tiān　　bù zhī dào wèi shén me　　jiā lǐ hū rán shōu dào chéng bǎi
有一天，不知道为什么，家里忽然收到成百
shàng qiān de xìn　　měi gè xìn fēng shàng dōu xiě zhe　　　　xiǎo tàn
上千的信。每个信封上都写着："Pili 小探
xiǎn jiā shōu
险家收。"

The envelopes had stamps from all over the planet. They came from the
North Pole and South Pole, from France and Russia, from China and India.
There were even hand-carried letters from the Galapagos Islands.

zhè xiē xìn fēng shàng yǒu lái zì shì jiè gè dì de yóu piào tā men yǒu xiē lái zì běi
这些信封上有来自世界各地的邮票。它们有些来自北
jí nán jí yǒu xiē lái zì fǎ guó é luó sī hái yǒu xiē lái zì zhōng guó hé yìn
极、南极，有些来自法国、俄罗斯，还有些来自中国和印
dù shèn zhì hái yǒu lǚ xíng zhě bāng máng cóng jiā lā bā gē qún dǎo dài lái de xìn
度。甚至还有旅行者帮忙从加拉巴哥群岛带来的信。

Where did all these letters come from?

"I've been telling everyone about your idea during all my travels and presentations," Pili's father said.

Pili could not contain her joy. "They all want to support my forest? Thank you so much, Dad. We're a team!"

这些信都是来自哪里的呢？

"我每次旅行和演讲的时候，都会把你的计划告诉大家，" Pili 的爸爸 Kikeo 说。

Pili 听了开心得不得了，"大家都支持我的森林计划是吗？太谢谢你了，爸爸！我们是一个团队！"

As they were taking off on their way to Colombia, Pili thought back on her adventure. "You may not have won the contest, but thanks to your idea and your work, the children of the world will always have their forest," said Kikeo.

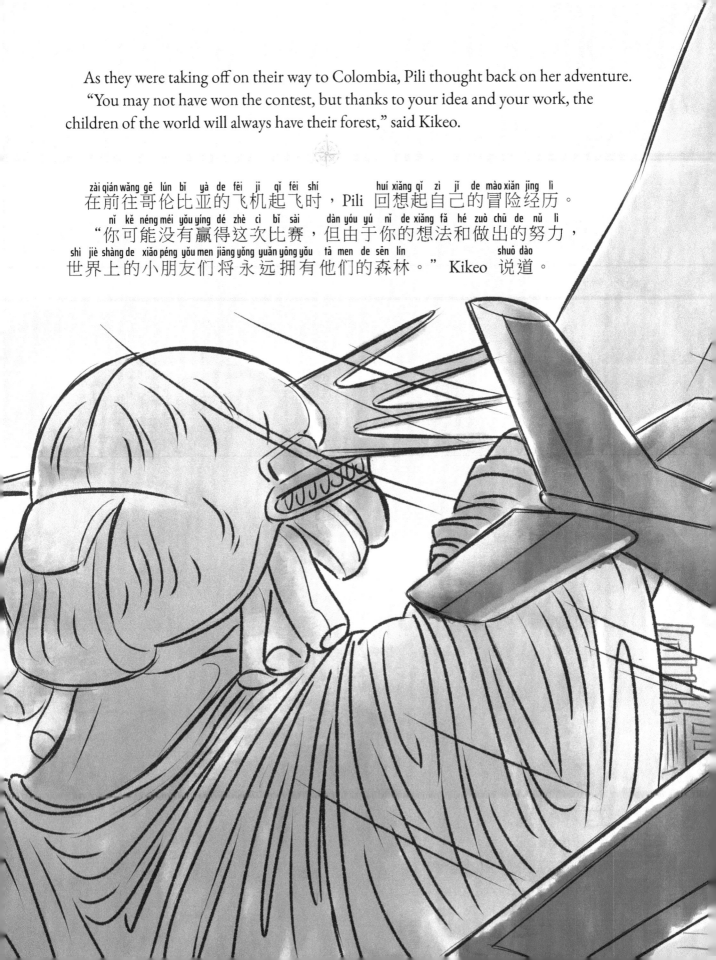

在前往哥伦比亚的飞机起飞时，Pili 回想起自己的冒险经历。
"你可能没有赢得这次比赛，但由于你的想法和做出的努力，
世界上的小朋友们将永远拥有他们的森林。" Kikeo 说道。

And that's how Pili, the little explorer, helped the world with one small action. It was just the beginning of many adventures for Pili and Kikeo as they traveled the world together.

Well done, Pili.

Well done, Dad.

THE END

zhè jiù shì xiǎo tàn xiǎn jiā 　　yòng tā de yí gè xiǎo xiǎo de xíng dòng bāng zhù
这就是小探险家 Pili 用她的一个小小的行动帮助
shì jiè de gù shi 　er zhè zhǐ shì 　　hé bà ba 　　zài yì qǐ huán
世界的故事。而这只是 Pili 和爸爸 Kikeo 在一起环
yóu shì jiè de mào xiǎn zhī lǚ de kāi shǐ
游世界的冒险之旅的开始。
zuò de hǎo
做得好，Pili。
zuò de hǎo 　bà ba
做得好，爸爸。

New York

What is Pili's favorite activity in New York?

Pili loves New York. Sometimes, exploring the city feels just like the trips she takes with her dad because she can meet people from around the world. She enjoys learning foreign languages, especially Chinese.

With her parents, she goes to parades and festivals that celebrate cultural diversity. Pili likes photographing the colorful costumes, while dancing to the rhythm of the music.

Are there any parades in your community that you would like to photograph?

zài niǔ yuē zuì xǐ huan de huó dòng shì shén me ne
Pili 在纽约最喜欢的活动是什么呢？

xǐ huan niǔ yuē yǒu shí hou tàn suǒ zhè zuò chéng shì jiù xiàng zài hé tā bà ba yì qǐ lǚ xíng yí yàng yīn wèi
Pili 喜欢纽约，有时候探索这座城市就像在和她爸爸一起旅行一样，因为

tā néng yù dào lái zì shì jiè gè dì de péng yǒu bìng qiě tā xǐ huan xué xí bù tóng de yǔ yán tè bié shì zhōng wén
她能遇到来自世界各地的朋友。并且她喜欢学习不同的语言，特别是中文。

zài fù mǔ de péi tóng xià tā chū qù tǐ yàn zhe yǒu zhe bù tóng wén huà de yóu xíng hé jié rì tā xǐ huan pāi
在父母的陪同下，她出去体验着有着不同文化的游行和节日。她喜欢拍

shè sè cǎi xiān yàn de fú shì tóng shí yě xǐ huan bàn suí zhe bù tóng jié zòu de yīn yuè wǔ dǎo
摄色彩鲜艳的服饰，同时也喜欢伴随着不同节奏的音乐舞蹈。

zài nǐ shēn biān zài nǐ shēng huó de huán jìng zhōng yǒu méi yǒu nǐ xiǎng pāi xià lái de yóu xíng hé huó dòng ne
在你身边，在你生活的环境中，有没有你想拍下来的游行和活动呢？

What is Pili's favorite place in New York?

Her favorite place in New York is Central Park. Pili is fascinated by its wildlife. Whenever she goes to Central Park, she brings along her binoculars and turns the walk into an urban safari.

"Look, Pili! It's Pale Male, the hawk who lives in the park," her dad said.

But sometimes Pili's curiosity gets her into trouble.

"I'll never forget the day we rescued flying squirrels and you decided to release them inside the apartment," her father said with a twinkle in his eye. "I had to chase them everywhere to take them to the animal shelter."

What kind of birds can you observe in your local park?

Pili 最喜欢纽约什么地方呢？

她最喜欢纽约的中央公园，她被那些野生动物们深深地吸引。无论什么时候去那里，她都会带上她的望远镜，就像去城市野生动物园一样。

"快看 Pili！是 Pale Male，那只生活在公园里的鹰，"她爸爸叫她。

但有时候 Pili 的好奇心会让她的父母陷入困境。

"我永远不会忘记我们救出飞鼠的那一天，你决定把它们放到我们家里，"她爸爸说。"我不得不到处追了它们几个小时，才把他们带到了动物收容所。"

在你们当地的公园里你能看到哪些鸟类呢？

What type of projects does Pili enjoying doing in New York?

In New York, people come from everywhere. Pili is always curious to learn how children live in other parts of the world.

"In Cuba, there are small urban gardens that are cared for by everyone, even the kids!" explained her father. "They grow tomatoes, carrots, and other healthy veggies."

We could do that, thought Pili. She rushed from door to door, telling her neighbors. And soon they had planted a small garden on the roof of their building.

Is there any area in your house, building or community where you would enjoy planting a vegetable garden?

Pili 在纽约喜欢做什么样的项目呢？
zài niǔ yuē xǐ huan zuò shén me yàng de xiàng mù ne

在纽约，人们来自各个不同的地方。Pili 总是对世界其
zài niǔ yuē rén men lái zì gè gè bù tóng de dì fāng zǒng shì duì shì jiè qí

他地方小朋友的生活方式感到很好奇。
tā dì fāng xiǎo péng yǒu de shēng huó fāng shì gǎn dào hěn hào qí

"在古巴有一些小花园，每个人都可以帮助照顾，
zài gǔ bā yǒu yì xiē xiǎo huā yuán měi gè rén dōu kě yǐ bāng zhù zhào gù

甚至小朋友也可以！"她爸爸告诉她。
shèn zhì xiǎo péng yǒu yě kě yǐ tā bà ba gào sù tā

"他们在公园里种番茄，胡萝卜和其他健康的蔬菜。"
tā men zài gōng yuán lǐ zhòng fān qié hú luó bo hé qí tā jiàn kāng de shū cài

我们也可以这样做，Pili 想。她开始挨家挨户告诉邻居
wǒ men yě kě yǐ zhè yàng zuò xiǎng tā kāi shǐ āi jiā āi hù gào sù lín jū

们她这个想法。于是很快他们一起在楼顶创造了一个小
men tā zhè ge xiǎng fǎ yú shì hěn kuài tā men yì qǐ zài lóu dǐng chuàng zào le yí gè xiǎo

花园。
huā yuán

在你们家，你们房子或社区里有你想要种菜种花的地方吗？
zài nǐ men jiā nǐ men fáng zi huò shè qū lǐ yǒu nǐ xiǎng yào zhòng cài zhòng huā de dì fāng ma

Suggested Keywords for Parents and Educators

jiàn yì fù mǔ hé lǎo shī kě yǐ shǐ yòng
建议父母和老师可以使用
de guān jiàn cí
的关键词

Family traditions – Pursuit of dreams
jiā tíng chuán tǒng　　zhuī xún mèng xiǎng
家庭传统 – 追寻梦想

Organic diet – Teasing and bullying
yǒu jī shí pǐn　　xué xiào qī líng
有机食品 – 学校欺凌

Empowerment – Global readiness
fù quán　　quán qiú jiào yù
赋权 – 全球教育

Entrepreneurship – Crowd funding
qǐ yè jiā jīng shén　　jí tǐ zhòng chóu
企业家精神 – 集体众筹

Courage – Adversity
yǒng qì　　nì jìng
勇气 – 逆境

Conflicting emotions – Perseverence
máo dùn de qíng xù　　jiān chí bú xiè
矛盾的情绪 – 坚持不懈

Cooperation – Globalization
hé zuò　　quán qiú huà
合作 – 全球化

Disappointment – Deadlines

shī wàng　　jié zhǐ rì qī

失望 – 截止日期

Handwritten letters – Pen Pals

shǒu xiě xìn　　bǐ yǒu

手写信 – 笔友

Teamwork – Parent-child teamwork

tuán duì hé zuò　　qīn zǐ tuán duì hé zuò

团队合作 – 亲子团队合作

Self-reflection – Optimism

zì wǒ fǎn xǐng　　lè guān

自我反省 – 乐观

Forest conservation – Climate Change

sēn lín bǎo hù　　qì hòu biàn huà

森林保护 – 气候变化

Cultural Diversity – Inclusion

wén huà duō yàng xìng　　bāo róng xìng

文化多样性 – 包容性

Urban wildlife – Birdwatching

chéng shì yě shēng dòng wù　　guān niǎo

城市野生动物 – 观鸟

Urban agriculture – Green roofs

chéng shì nóng yè　　lǜ sè wū dǐng

城市农业 – 绿色屋顶